A minedition book
published by Penguin Young Readers Group

Text and Illustrations copyright © 2005 by Eve Tharlet
Coproduction with Michael Neugebauer Publishing Ltd. Hong Kong
All rights reserved. This book, or parts thereof, may not be reproduced
in any form without permission in writing from the publisher,
Penguin Young Readers Group,
345 Hudson Street, New York, NY 10014.
The scanning, uploading and distribution of this book via the Internet or via
any other means without the permission of the publisher is illegal and pun-
ishable by law. Please purchase only authorized electronic editions,
and do not participate in or encourage electronic piracy of copyrighted mate-
rials. Your support of the author's rights is appreciated.
Published simultaneously in Canada.
Manufactured in Hong Kong by Wide World Ltd.
Designed by Michael Neugebauer
Typesetting in R Stempel Garamond
Color separation by Fotoreproduzioni Grafiche, Verona, Italy.

Library of Congress Cataloging-in-Publication Data available upon request.
ISBN 0-698-40008-9

10 9 8 7 6 5 4 3 2 1
First Impression

For more information please visit our website: www.minedition.com

Translated by Charise Myngheer

Nancy, the Little Gosling

Written and Illustrated by
Eve Tharlet

minedition

"Get in single file. It's time to waddle across the field!"
announced Mrs. Green. "Left foot first. And begin!
Left-two-three-four,
left-two-three-four…"
All the little goslings waddled behind her.
Well, not all of them.
Little Nancy just stood and watched.
She didn't know which foot she should
move first. Was it her left one?
Or was it her other left one?

Then she saw something.
Oh, what a beautiful butterfly!
Nancy had never seen one like it.
"Nanc---*eee*," called Mrs. Green loudly. "What's taking you so long?
You're always the last one."
All the little goslings nodded and cackled together, "Come on Nancy.
It's time for our flying lesson!"

"You know what to do," said Mrs. Green.
"Flap both wings the same. And then stretch your legs out
and land."
  One after the other, the little goslings flew across the field.
"And now it's your turn, Nancy!" called all the other goslings.
  Nancy took a running start and staggered into the air.
  Flap, flap, flap…
  Hey, there's that butterfly again!
  Nancy watched it excitedly.
  Flap, flap, flap…

SPLAT!
Nancy landed with a somersault.
Lucky for her, the grass was tall and soft.
"Nancy, what were you looking at?"
sighed Mrs. Green. "Did you hurt yourself?"
Nancy shook her head.
"Good work kids," said Mrs. Green. "That's
all for today. Tomorrow morning we'll meet
for your swimming lesson!"

"What? Swimming, too?" thought Nancy unhappily
as she waddled home.

"What's wrong?" asked her mother when she saw
Nancy's sad face.

"Oh, Mom, I can't do anything right!" complained
Nancy. "Not waddle, not fly, and especially not swim!"

"Hmm, I'm sure it's not that bad," said Mama
Goose. "What would you like to be when
you grow up?"

"A butterfly researcher!" answered Nancy
excitedly.

"Well then, you do need to learn how to do
these things," said Mama Goose. "Or you won't
be able to keep up with the butterflies."

That night Nancy couldn't sleep. She didn't know what to do.
She knew she could practice waddling and flying, but stupid swimming…
If only she didn't have to learn how to swim!
*I don't like water. But I can't tell anyone, because they would just
laugh at me. Who ever heard of a gosling that doesn't like to swim?
It even sounds ridiculous to me!*

Nancy sighed. *It's hopeless!
I'll never be a great butterfly researcher…*

The next morning, the goslings gathered along the shore cackling.
Everybody was excited about the swimming lesson.
"Swimming is my favorite," Lucy said excitedly.
All the other little goslings called out, "Mine too!"
Well, not all of them.
Little Nancy shivered. Slowly she put her toes
into the water.
"Brrrrr, it's cold! And so wet!" she exclaimed.

Mrs. Green waddled to the front of the group.
"Okay everyone," she said. "Jump in.
Remember, one behind the other.
And Nancy, you can watch. Now pay attention."
So Nancy stood there and watched.
But she didn't pay attention for long…

There it was again... the butterfly!
Nancy jumped for joy.
"Oh, I have to see it close up.
But how can I get to it?"
Then Nancy spotted a lily pad and said,
"That would work!"

Before anyone realized what was happening,
Nancy flitted across the water.
"Mrs. Green!" all the little goslings called out.
"Look at how fast Nancy can swim!"
They all watched in amazement as Nancy skillfully surfed across
the water on the lily pad.

Just before she reached it, she gently slowed down and
made a beautiful curve around the butterfly so she
wouldn't frighten it.

And for the first time, she saw the butterfly close up.
"You're really wonderful," she said.
"If I'm the first one to find you, I'll give you a name.
I will call you Lepidoptera Nancy."

When the butterfly flew away, Nancy happily surfed back to shore.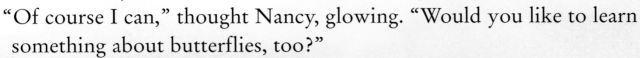
"Bravo, Nancy!" shouted the goslings as they flapped their wings excitedly. "That was fantastic! How did you learn how to do that?"
"How? What?" Nancy was confused. "Oh, you mean leaf surfing!"
"Yeah! Can you teach us how? Please!" the goslings asked.
"Of course I can," thought Nancy, glowing. "Would you like to learn something about butterflies, too?"

The rest of the day was lots of fun.
Everyone learned something from little Nancy.
Everyone?
Yes, everyone!